BAT'S BIG GAME

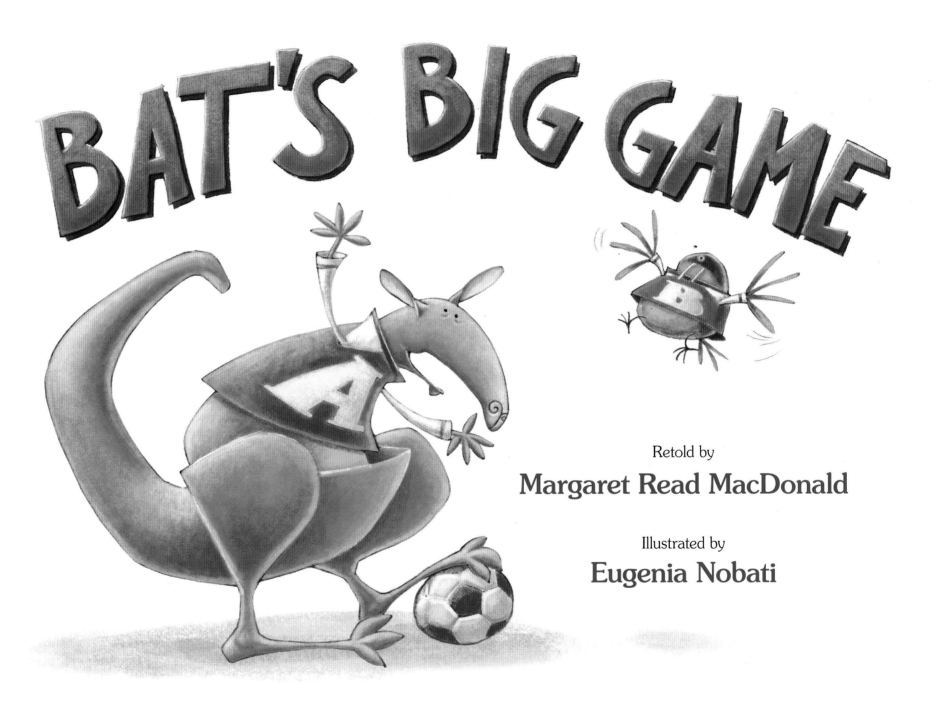

Retold by

Margaret Read MacDonald

Illustrated by

Eugenia Nobati

Albert Whitman & Company, Morton Grove, Illinois

For Cordelia's Daddy Nat and her Uncle Tom, who help me read and read these texts until they sound just right.—M.R.M.

For my two great advisors: my son, Luciano, and my husband, Alejandro—E.N.

About This Tale

The earliest versions of this tale seem to be from Aesop. *(Motif B261.1 Bat in war between birds and quadrupeds. Bat joins first one side then another. He is discredited by both the birds and the quadrupeds for his double-dealing actions.)* Stith Thompson's *Motif-Index to Folk-Literature* mentions also sources from the Benga, Ibo, Yoruba, and Mgongwe peoples, as well as from India and Japan. Sometimes the tale has a different ending. My *Storyteller's Sourcebook* cites an Upper Volta version in which Bat refuses to fight with either side. In several Native American variants, a stickball game is taking place. In a Cree tale, Bat makes a winning catch for the animals and is accepted by them. In Creek (Muskogee) and Cherokee variants, Bat makes a winning catch for the birds. The birds have made wings for Bat, who did not have them, so he can join their side.

Library of Congress Cataloging-in-Publication Data

MacDonald, Margaret Read, 1940-
Bat's big game / retold by Margaret Read MacDonald ; illustrated by Eugenia Nobati.
p. cm.
Summary: A simplified retelling of the classic Aesop's fable about a ball game between the birds
and the animals, and Bat, who wants to play on the winning team.
ISBN 978-0-8075-0587-8 (hardcover)
[1. Fables. 2. Loyalty—Fiction. 3. Folklore.] I. Nobati, Eugenia, ill. II. Aesop. III. Title.
PZ8.2.M16Bat 2008 398.2—dc22 [E] 2007030929

The design is by Carol Gildar.
The illustrations were created digitally.

For information about Albert Whitman & Company, please visit our web site at www.albertwhitman.com

The Animals and the Birds decided to have a ball game.
The Animals came onto the field first.
They had big blue shirts with a great big "A."

Bear put his shirt on and paraded around.

He was strong.

Deer put her shirt on and got ready to run down the field.

She was fast.

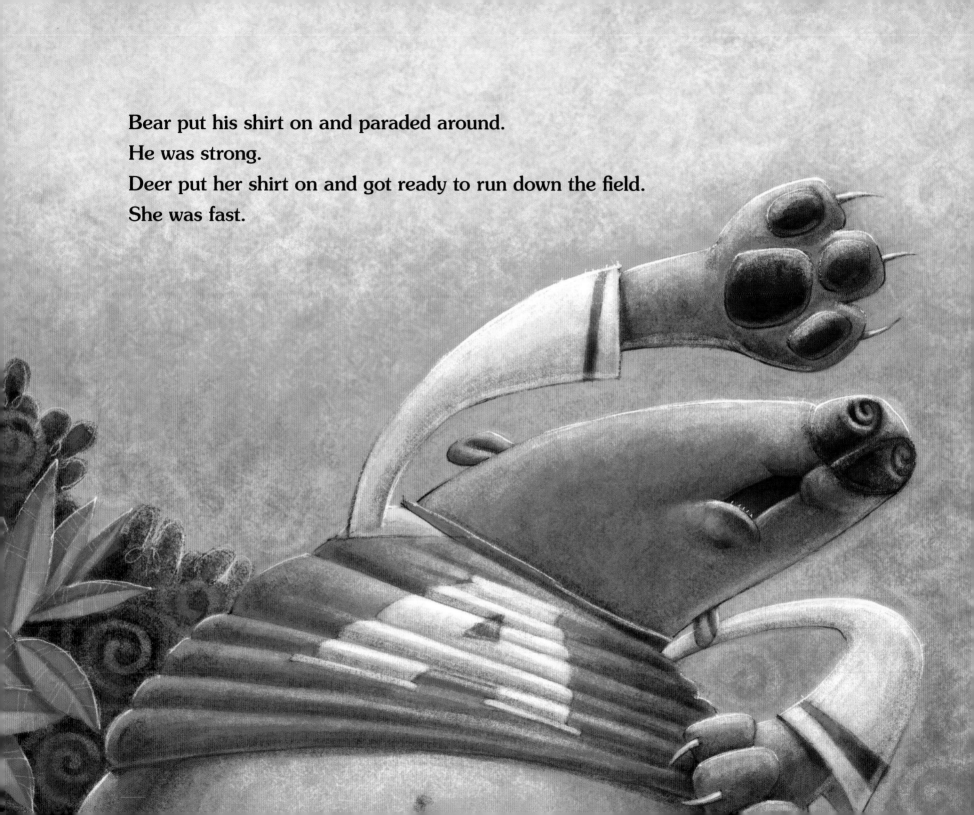

Kangaroo put her shirt on and practiced her kicks.
If she got the ball, she would just drop it in her pouch,
   hop down the field, and kick a goal!
The Animals were exercising and stretching out,
   getting ready for the big game.

At the other end of the field, the Birds began to arrive.
Sparrow came. Wren and Robin flew in.
Big Birds, too—Eagle and Ostrich.
Ostrich couldn't fly, but if she got the ball in her beak
    she could *run*.

The Birds all had little red shirts with a little "B."
They put on their shirts and stretched their wings,
    getting ready for the big game!

"We're the BIRDS!
Look at that B!
Birds are gonna win!
B! B! B!"

At the other end of the field, the Animals were ready to go.

"We're the ANIMALS!

Look at that A!

Animals gonna win!

A! A! A!"

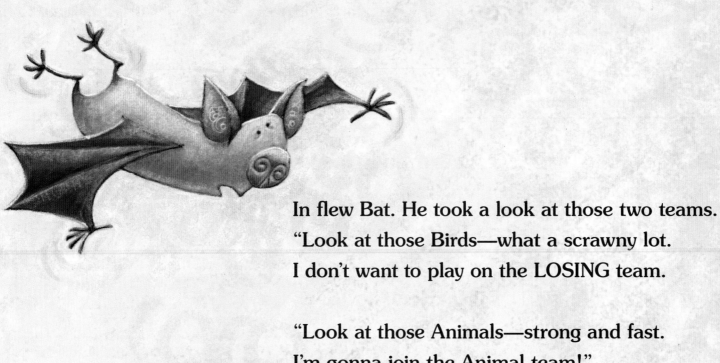

In flew Bat. He took a look at those two teams.
"Look at those Birds—what a scrawny lot.
I don't want to play on the LOSING team.

"Look at those Animals—strong and fast.
I'm gonna join the Animal team!"

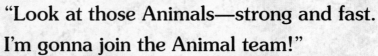

"Here I am, cousins! Where's my shirt?
I'm ready to play on the Animal team!"
The Animals looked Bat over. "Are you an Animal?"
"What's that folded behind your back? Are those *wings?*"

"Sure, I'm an Animal," said Bat.
"Look at these teeth! Do birds have teeth?
Feel this fur. Do birds have *fur?*
OF COURSE I'm an Animal!"

So the Animals gave Bat a shirt with an "A."

Bat jumped up and down, shouting,

"Go Animals! Gonna win this game!
GO! GO! GO!
I'm on the winning side!"

And the game started!
Bear kicked the ball down the field and made a goal.

Then Sparrow took the ball and flew down
the field and made a goal.

Then Deer kicked the ball down the field . . . but Robin snatched it!

Robin flew down the field and made another goal!
And the Birds were winning, 2 to 1.

"Uh, oh," said Bat. "Looks like I made a mistake.
I'm on the *losing* side! I should have joined the Bird team."
Bat took off his Animal shirt and hung it on a bush.

He tiptoed down the field to the Birds' side.
"Hi there, cousins! I've come to join the game!
Where's my shirt? Looks like we're gonna win!"

The Birds looked Bat over. "We didn't know you were a Bird.
Weren't you playing for the Animals a minute ago?"
"I'm no Animal," said Bat. "Look at these wings!
Do Animals have wings? OF COURSE I'm a Bird!"

So the Birds gave Bat a shirt with a B.

"Go Birds! Gonna win this game!
GO! GO! GO!
I'm on the winning side!"

The game started again.
Wren got the ball
and flew down the field
and made a goal.

Deer got the ball
and ran down the field
and made a goal.

Eagle took the ball and flew down the field and dropped it,
and Kangaroo kicked the ball and she made a goal!

Now the Animals had the ball.
Raccoon passed to Kangaroo. Kangaroo kicked another goal!
And the Animals were leading, 4-3!

"Uh, oh," thought Bat. "These Birds are losing.
I'd better switch back to the Animal team."
Bat took off his Bird shirt and hung it on a bush.
He tiptoed up the field . . . put on his Animal shirt . . .
    and ran back into the game, shouting,

"Go Animals! Gonna win this game! GO! GO! GO! I'm on the winning side!"

"Wait a minute!" Bear stopped the game.
"Eagle, bring your Birds over here.
Animals, you all come here!"

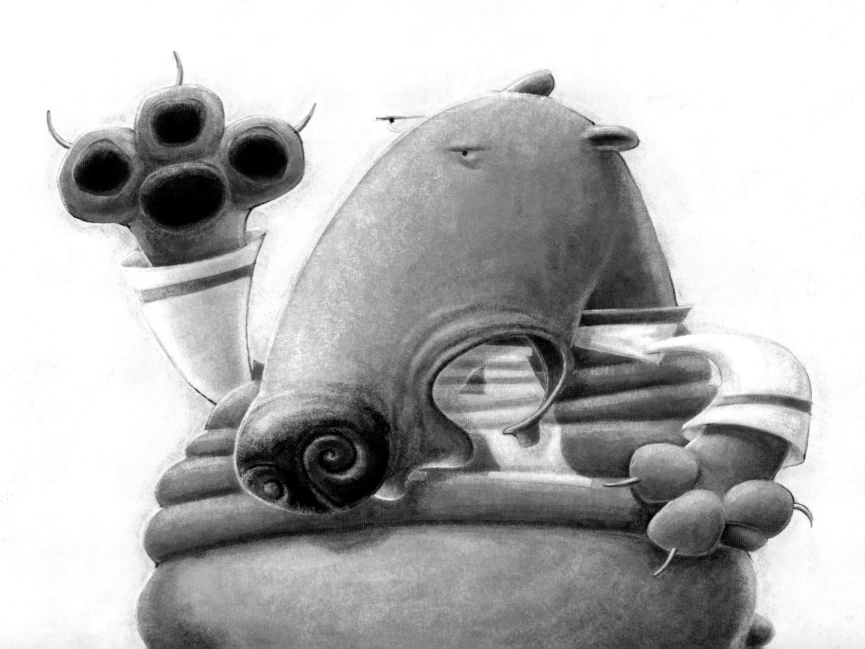

"Look at this Bat.

Wasn't he playing on the Bird team a minute ago?"

"Yes . . . he was," said the Birds.

"And wasn't he playing on the Animal team a while ago?" asked Bear.

"Yes . . . he was," said the Animals.

"Well, Bat, which side are you on? Are you a Bird or an Animal?"

Everyone waited.

"Well . . . I just wanted to play on the winning side," mumbled Bat.

"I'm sorry for you, Bat," said Bear. "But a good player sticks with the
team . . . even when they are *losing*.

Looks like you are not on *any* side now."

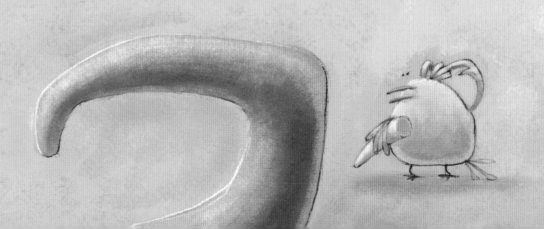

Bat gave back the shirt with the "A."
Bat gave back the shirt with the "B."

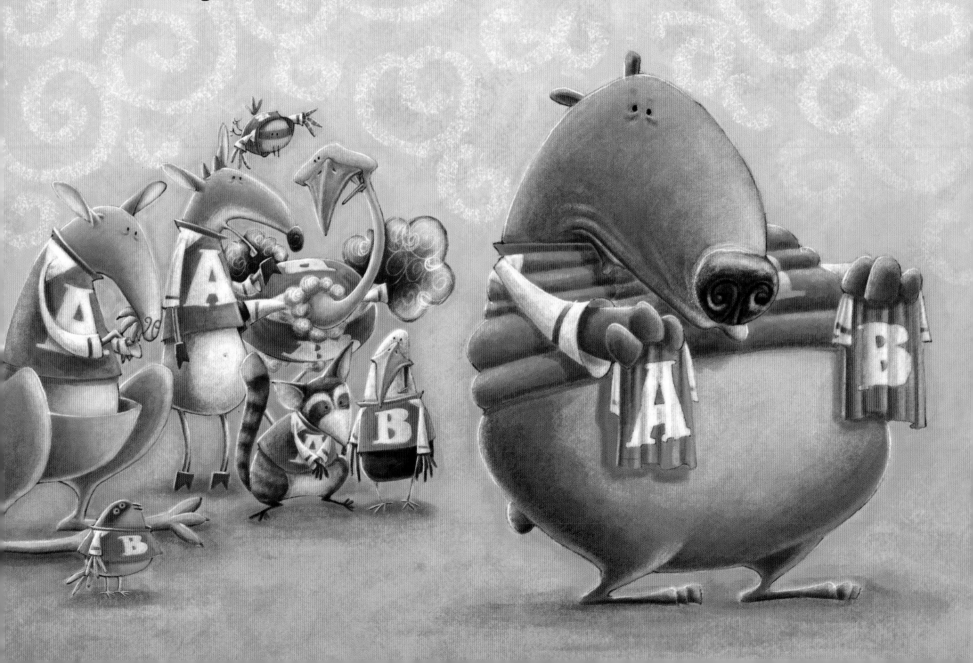

And Bat left the field.

"BAT WANTS TO WIN...
GO ... GO ... GO!"

They say Bat is still practicing his game.

I'm not sure which side he plans to play on.

But that's the last time he'll play both sides at once!